Ricky Ricotta's Mighty Robot Adventures

Three Adventures by
DAV PILKEY
Pictures by
MARTIN ONTIVEROS

SCHOLASTIC INC.

New York Toronto London Auckland Sydney
Mexico City New Delhi Hong Kong Buenos Aires

For information regarding permission, please write to: Permissions Department, Scholastic Inc., 557 Broadway, New York, NY 10012.

12 11 10 9 8 7 6 5 4 3 2 1   5 6 7 8 9 10/0

Printed in the United States of America   40

This edition created exclusively for Barnes & Noble, Inc. 2005 Barnes & Noble Books

ISBN 0-7607-9592-4

This edition first printing, September 2005

CONTENTS

Ricky Ricotta's Mighty Robot

Originally published as RICKY RICOTTA'S GIANT ROBOT

For Walter Bain Wills — D. P.

*To my mom and my family, to all of my friends everywhere
(you know who you are), for their love and support,
and most of all to Micki, and our two kitties,
Bunny and Spanky — M. O.*

Chapters

CHAPTER 1

Ricky

There once was a mouse named Ricky Ricotta who lived in Squeakyville with his mother and father.

Ricky liked living with
his mother and father, but
sometimes he got lonely.

Ricky wished he had a friend
to keep him company.

"Don't worry," said Ricky's father.
"Some day something **BIG** will
happen, and you will find a friend."
So Ricky waited.

CHAPTER 2

The Bullies

Ricky liked school, but he
did not like walking to school.
This was because Ricky was
very small, and sometimes
bullies picked on him.

"Where do you think you are going?" asked one of the bullies.

Ricky did not answer. He
turned and started to run.

The bullies chased him.

They knocked Ricky down
and threw his backpack
into a garbage can.

Every day, the bullies chased Ricky.
Every day, they knocked him down.
And every day, Ricky wished that
something **BIG** would happen.

CHAPTER 3

Dr. Stinky McNasty

That day at school, Ricky
ate lunch by himself. Then
he went outside for recess.

He watched the other mice
play a game of kickball.
Ricky did not know that
something **BIG** was about
to happen, but it *was*!

In a secret cave above
the city, a mad doctor was
planning something evil.

Dr. Stinky McNasty had
created a Mighty Robot.

"I will use this Robot to destroy the city," said Dr. Stinky, "and soon, I will rule the world!"

Dr. Stinky led his Mighty Robot into town.

"Robot," said Dr. Stinky, "I want you to **jump** and **stomp** and ***destroy this city***!"

CHAPTER 4

The Mighty Robot

(IN FLIP-O-RAMA™)

⊃·RAMA

HERE'S HOW IT WORKS!

STEP 1
Place your *left* hand inside the dotted lines marked "LEFT HAND HERE." Hold the book open *flat*.

STEP 2
Grasp the *right-hand* page with your right thumb and index finger (inside the dotted lines marked "RIGHT THUMB HERE").

STEP 3
Now *quickly* flip the right-hand page back and forth until the picture appears to be *animated*.

(For extra fun, try adding your own sound-effects!)

FLIP-O-RAMA 1

(pages 29 and 31)

Remember, flip *only* page 29.
While you are flipping, be sure
you can see the picture on page 29
and the one on page 31.
If you flip quickly, the two
pictures will start to look like
<u>one</u> *animated* picture.

Don't forget to add
your own sound-effects!

LEFT HAND HERE

The Robot Jumped.

RIGHT
THUMB
HERE

The Robot Jumped.

FLIP-O-RAMA 2

(pages 33 and 35)

Remember, flip *only* page 33.
While you are flipping, be sure
you can see the picture on page 33
and the one on page 35.
If you flip quickly, the two
pictures will start to look like
<u>one</u> *animated* picture.

Don't forget to add
your own sound-effects!

LEFT HAND HERE

The Robot Stomped.

RIGHT
THUMB
HERE

The Robot Stomped.

FLIP-O-RAMA 3

(pages 37 and 39)

Remember, flip *only* page 37.
While you are flipping, be sure
you can see the picture on page 37
and the one on page 39.
If you flip quickly, the two
pictures will start to look like
<u>one</u> *animated* picture.

Don't forget to add
your own sound-effects!

LEFT HAND HERE

But the Robot Would Not Destroy the City.

RIGHT THUMB HERE

But the Robot Would Not Destroy the City.

CHAPTER 5

Ricky to the Rescue

Dr. Stinky was very angry.
"Destroy Squeakyville!" he
cried. "Destroy Squeakyville!"
But the Robot refused.

"I will teach you a lesson,"
said Dr. Stinky. He pressed
a button on his remote control
and zapped the Robot with
a terrible shock.

Ricky was watching.

"Stop it!" Ricky cried. But Dr.
Stinky kept on zapping the Robot.

Finally, Ricky aimed a kickball
at the evil doctor. Ricky kicked
as hard as he could.

BOING!

The kickball bounced off Dr. Stinky's head. Dr. Stinky dropped the controller, and it broke on the ground.

"Rats! Rats! *RATS!*" cried Dr. Stinky. "I shall return!" And he disappeared down a sewer drain.

When the Robot saw what Ricky
had done, he walked over to Ricky.
Everyone screamed and ran.

But Ricky was not afraid. The
Robot smiled and patted Ricky
on the head.

Something **BIG** had happened
after all!

CHAPTER 6
Ricky's Pet Robot

That afternoon, the Robot followed
Ricky home from school.

Soon they got to Ricky's
house. "Wait here, Robot," said
Ricky. Ricky went inside.

"Mom, Dad," said Ricky, "can I have a pet?"

"Well," said Ricky's father, "you've been a good mouse lately."

"Yes," said Ricky's mother, "I think a pet would be good for you."

"Hooray!" said Ricky.
"Uh-oh," said Ricky's parents.

CHAPTER 7

Ricky's Mighty Robot Helps Out

When Ricky's parents saw Ricky's new pet, they were not happy.

"That Robot is too big to be a pet," said Ricky's father.

"There is no room for him in our home," said Ricky's mom.

"But he is my friend,"
said Ricky, "and he will
help us around the house!"

Ricky's Mighty Robot used his super breath to blow all the leaves out of their yard. Ricky's dad liked that.

Ricky's Robot scared all the crows
out of the vegetable garden.
Ricky's mom liked that.

And when burglars drove
by the Ricottas' house,
they kept right on driving.
Everybody liked that!

"Well," said Ricky's father,
"I guess your Robot can live
in the garage."
"Hooray!" said Ricky.

CHAPTER 8

Back to School

The next day, Ricky and his Robot walked to school. The bullies were waiting for Ricky.

"Where do you think you're going?" asked one of the bullies.

"My Robot and I are going to school," said Ricky.

The bullies looked up and saw Ricky's Mighty Robot. They were very frightened.

"Um . . . um . . . um . . ." said
one of the bullies, "can we carry
your backpack for you, sir?"

"Sure," said Ricky.

The bullies helped Ricky get to
school safely.

"Is there anything else we can
do for you, sir?" asked the bullies.

"No, thank you," said Ricky.

CHAPTER 9

Show-and-Tell

That day at school, Ricky's class had show-and-tell. One mouse brought a baseball glove. Another mouse brought a teddy bear.

Ricky brought his Mighty Robot.

Ricky's class got a free
ride on the Robot's back.

They flew up above the city
and over the mountains.

"This is fun!" said Ricky.

CHAPTER 10

Dr. Stinky's Revenge

While Ricky's class was flying around in the sky, Dr. Stinky sneaked over to the school. He wanted revenge!

Dr. Stinky crept into Ricky's classroom. He saw their pet lizard.

"This is just what I need!" said Dr. Stinky.

He took out a bottle of Hate
Potion #9 and put a drop
into the lizard's water dish.
The lizard drank the water.

Suddenly, the lizard began to grow and change. He got bigger and bigger. He got meaner and meaner.

Soon, the lizard turned into
an evil monster.

"Destroy Ricky and his Robot!"
said Dr. Stinky.

"Yes, Master!" said the monster.

When Ricky's Robot saw
the evil monster, he flew down
to the schoolyard. Ricky and
his class climbed off quickly.
Then, the Robot turned toward
the giant monster, and the
battle began.

CHAPTER 11

The Big Battle

(IN FLIP-O-RAMA™)

FLIP-O-RAMA 4

(pages 77 and 79)

Remember, flip *only* page 77.
While you are flipping, be sure
you can see the picture on page 77
and the one on page 79.
If you flip quickly, the two
pictures will start to look like
<u>one</u> *animated* picture.

Don't forget to add
your own sound-effects!

LEFT HAND HERE

The Monster
Attacked.

RIGHT
THUMB
HERE

The Monster
Attacked.

FLIP-O-RAMA 5

(pages 81 and 83)

Remember, flip *only* page 81.
While you are flipping, be sure
you can see the picture on page 81
and the one on page 83.
If you flip quickly, the two
pictures will start to look like
<u>one</u> *animated* picture.

Don't forget to add
your own sound-effects!

LEFT HAND HERE

Ricky's Robot
Fought Back.

82

Ricky's Robot
Fought Back.

FLIP-O-RAMA 6

(pages 85 and 87)

Remember, flip *only* page 85.
While you are flipping, be sure
you can see the picture on page 85
and the one on page 87.
If you flip quickly, the two
pictures will start to look like
<u>one</u> *animated* picture.

Don't forget to add
your own sound-effects!

LEFT HAND HERE

The Monster
Battled Hard.

RIGHT
THUMB
HERE

The Monster
Battled Hard.

FLIP-O-RAMA 7

(pages 89 and 91)

Remember, flip *only* page 89.
While you are flipping, be sure
you can see the picture on page 89
and the one on page 91.
If you flip quickly, the two
pictures will start to look like
<u>one</u> *animated* picture.

Don't forget to add
your own sound-effects!

LEFT HAND HERE

Ricky's Robot
Battled Harder.

RIGHT
THUMB
HERE

Ricky's Robot
Battled Harder.

FLIP-O-RAMA 8

(pages 93 and 95)

Remember, flip *only* page 93.
While you are flipping, be sure
you can see the picture on page 93
and the one on page 95.
If you flip quickly, the two
pictures will start to look like
<u>one</u> *animated* picture.

Don't forget to add
your own sound-effects!

LEFT HAND HERE

Ricky's Robot
Saved the Day.

RIGHT
THUMB
HERE

Ricky's Robot
Saved the Day.

CHAPTER 12

The Electro-Rocket

The monster was defeated, and all of his evil powers went away. Soon, he turned back into a tiny lizard and never bothered anybody again.

"Rats! Rats! *RATS!*" cried Dr. Stinky. "I will destroy that Robot myself!" He took his Electro-Rocket and aimed it at Ricky's Robot.

"NO!" screamed Ricky. He
leaped onto Dr. Stinky just as
the evil doctor fired his rocket.

Up, up, up went the rocket.
Ricky's Robot flew after it.
But he was not fast enough.

The rocket came down and
exploded.

Ka-BOOM!

Right on Dr. Stinky's secret cave.

CHAPTER 13

Justice Prevails

"Rats! Rats! *RATS!*" cried Dr. Stinky. "This has been a bad day for me!"

"It is about to get worse," said Ricky.

Ricky's Mighty Robot
picked up Dr. Stinky and
put him in the city jail.

CHAPTER 14

Back Home

That night, the Ricotta family
had a cookout in the backyard.
Ricky told his mom and dad all
about their adventures that day.

"Thank you for saving the city," said Ricky's father.

"And thank you for saving each other," said Ricky's mother.

"No problem," said Ricky . . .

HOW TO DRAW RICKY'S ROBOT

1.

2.
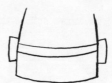

3.

4.

5.

6.

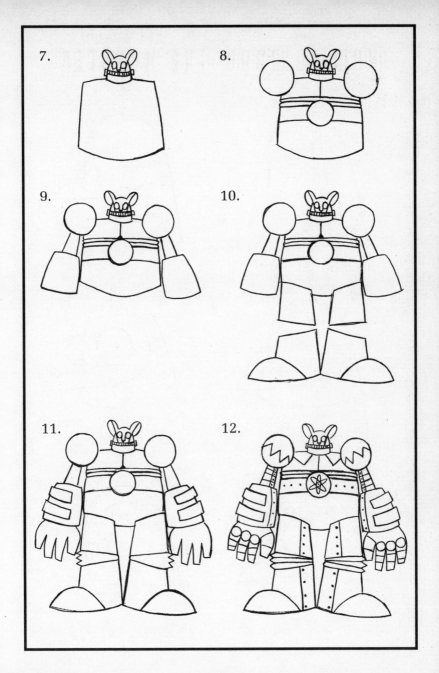

HOW TO DRAW THE MONSTER

1.

2.

3.

4.

5.

6.

Ricky Ricotta's Mighty Robot vs. the Mutant Mosquitoes from Mercury

Originally published as RICKY RICOTTA'S GIANT ROBOT VS. THE MUTANT MOSQUITOES FROM MERCURY

For Robbie Staenberg — D. P.

To Micki, Derek, Bwana, Marny,
Alicia, Craig, Kalah, JP,
and my cats — M. O.

Chapters

CHAPTER 1

Ricky and His Robot

There once was a mouse named Ricky Ricotta who lived in Squeakyville with his mother and father.

Ricky Ricotta might have been
the smallest mouse around . . .

. . . but he had the BIGGEST
best friend in town.

CHAPTER 2

School Days

Ricky and his Mighty Robot
liked to go to school together.

Sometimes when Ricky was running late, his Robot would fly him straight to the front door.

After school, the Mighty Robot liked
to help Ricky with his homework.
The Robot's computer brain could
solve complex math problems . . .

. . . his finger had a built-in
pencil sharpener . . .

. . . and he could even remove his telescopic eyeball, which made studying the planets much easier.

"Wow," said Ricky. "I can see all
the way to Mercury! That's cool!"

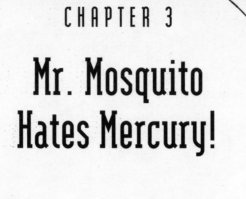

CHAPTER 3

Mr. Mosquito Hates Mercury!

Mercury was the smallest planet in the solar system, and it was the closest planet to the sun. But it certainly was not *cool*!

Just ask Mr. Mosquito. He lived on Mercury, and he HATED everything about it!

He hated the long, *long,* HOT days. Each day on Mercury, the temperature rose to more than eight hundred degrees!

Mr. Mosquito couldn't even walk down the street because his flip-flops always melted on the sidewalk.

Mr. Mosquito hated Mercury's long, *long,* COLD nights, too. Each night on Mercury, the temperature dropped to almost three hundred degrees below zero!

Mr. Mosquito couldn't
even brush his teeth because
his toothpaste was always
frozen solid!

"I've g-g-got to g-g-get away f-f-from th-th-this awful p-p-planet," said Mr. Mosquito, shivering in the cold. So Mr. Mosquito looked through his telescope and saw the planet Earth.

He saw mice playing happily on cool autumn days.

He saw them sleeping soundly on
warm summer nights.

"Earth is the planet for me!" said
Mr. Mosquito. "Soon it will be mine!"

CHAPTER 4

Mr. Mosquito Makes His Move

Mr. Mosquito went into his secret laboratory and clipped his filthy fingernails.

He put the clippings into
a giant machine and zapped
them with a powerful ray.

Then, Mr. Mosquito's fingernails
grew and grew and grew . . .

... into massive Mutant Mosquitoes!

Mr. Mosquito climbed aboard his
spaceship and called to his troops.
"Mutant Mosquitoes," he cried,
"it is time to conquer Earth!
Follow me!"

And they did.

CHAPTER 5

The Mosquitoes Attack

When Mr. Mosquito got to Earth, he ordered his Mutant Mosquitoes to attack Squeakyville.

Ricky was in math class that afternoon. He looked out the window and saw the Mutant Mosquitoes.

"Uh-oh," said Ricky. "It looks like Squeakyville needs our help!"

Ricky raised his hand.

"May I be excused?" Ricky asked his teacher. "My Robot and I have to save the Earth."

"Not until you've finished your math test," said Ricky's teacher.

Ricky had three problems left. "What is two times three?" he asked himself aloud.

Ricky's Robot was waiting outside. He wanted to help. So he dashed to the teachers' parking lot and brought back some cars.

Ricky's Robot put three cars into one pile, and he put three cars into another pile.

Ricky looked at the piles of cars.
"*Two* piles of *three* cars," said
Ricky. "Two times three equals *six*!"

Ricky looked at his next question.
"What is *six* minus *five*?" he asked.
Ricky's Robot knew just what to do.

He threw five of the cars
back into the parking lot.

"I get it," said Ricky. "Six
minus five equals *one*!"

Ricky's last question was the hardest of all.

"What is *one* divided by *two*?" he asked.

The Robot used his mighty karate chop to divide one car in two.

"That was easy," said Ricky. "One divided by two equals *one-half*!"

Ricky handed in his test. Then
he climbed out the window.

"Let's go, Mighty Robot," said
Ricky. "We've got to save the Earth."

"M-m-m-my *car*!" cried Ricky's
teacher.

CHAPTER 6

The Heroes Arrive

Ricky and his Mighty Robot
ran downtown to face the
Mutant Mosquitoes.

The Mosquitoes attacked Ricky's Robot.

"Hey," said Ricky. "Four against one is not fair!"

Then Ricky had an idea.

"Come with me, Robot," said Ricky.

The Mighty Robot was busy fighting, so he could not follow Ricky. But his arm could stretch very far!

Ricky and his Robot's arm
stretched all the way to the
"Bugs Away" bug-spray factory.
Ricky told the Robot's arm to
grab one of the huge bug-spray
storage tanks.

Then they headed back to the battle.

CHAPTER 7
A Buggy Battle

The Robot shook the
tank of bug spray.

The Robot sprayed the Mosquitoes.

Then he broke up the buggy
battle with a big blast from
his bionic boot!

CHAPTER 8

Mr. Mosquito's Revenge

The Mutant Mosquitoes had been defeated. Ricky's Mighty Robot chased them into space.

The Mosquitoes flew
back to Mercury and never
bothered anybody again.

Mr. Mosquito was very angry. He grabbed Ricky and took him into his spaceship. "Help me, Robot," Ricky cried.

But it was too late. Mr. Mosquito
chained Ricky up. Then he went
to his control panel and pulled a
secret lever.

Suddenly his spaceship began
to change. It shifted . . .

. . . and grew . . .

. . . and transformed into a giant
Mecha-Mosquito!

The Mecha-Mosquito attacked
Ricky's Mighty Robot. But Ricky's
Robot would not fight back.

He knew that Ricky was inside the Mecha-Mosquito, and he did not want his best friend to get hurt.

The Mecha-Mosquito
pounded Ricky's Robot.

What could Ricky do?

Ricky thought and thought.

Then he had an idea.

"Mr. Mosquito," said Ricky,

"I have to go to the bathroom."

"Not now," said Mr. Mosquito.
"I am too busy beating up
your Robot!"

"But it's an emergency," said Ricky.

"Alright, alright," said Mr.
Mosquito. He unlocked Ricky's chains
and led him to the boys' room.

"Hurry up in there!" he yelled.

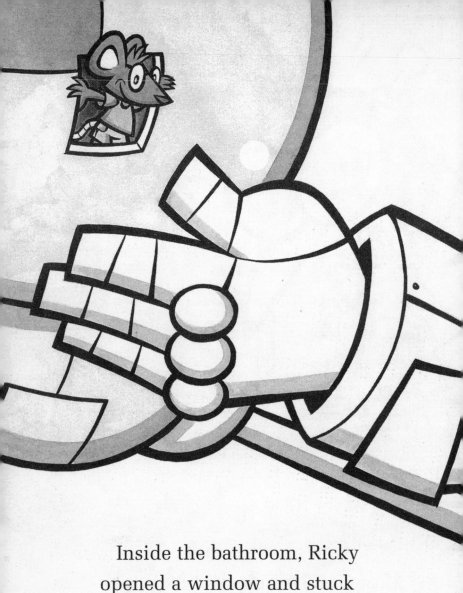

Inside the bathroom, Ricky
opened a window and stuck
his head outside.

"Pssssst!" Ricky whispered.

The Robot saw Ricky, and
he held out his giant hand.

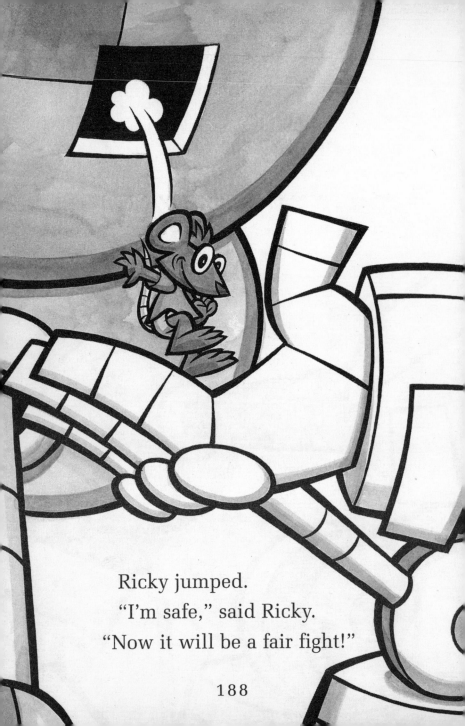

Ricky jumped.

"I'm safe," said Ricky.

"Now it will be a fair fight!"

CHAPTER 9

Ricky's Robot Strikes Back

Inside the Mecha-Mosquito, Mr. Mosquito was getting very angry. He knocked on the bathroom door. "Let's hurry up in there!" he yelled. "I haven't got all da—"

KER-POW!

Ricky's Robot punched the
Mecha-Mosquito right in the face.

Mr. Mosquito leaped to his
control panel and fought back hard.
The final battle was about to begin.

192

CHAPTER 10

The Final Battle

(IN FLIP-O-RAMA™)

⋯-RAMA

HERE'S HOW IT WORKS!

STEP 1
Place your *left* hand inside the dotted lines marked "LEFT HAND HERE." Hold the book open *flat*.

STEP 2
Grasp the *right-hand* page with your right thumb and index finger (inside the dotted lines marked "RIGHT THUMB HERE").

STEP 3
Now *quickly* flip the right-hand page back and forth until the picture appears to be *animated*.

(For extra fun, try adding your own sound-effects!)

FLIP-O-RAMA 1

(pages 197 and 199)

Remember, flip *only* page 197.
While you are flipping, be sure
you can see the picture on page 197
and the one on page 199.
If you flip quickly, the two
pictures will start to look like
<u>one</u> *animated* picture.

Don't forget to add
your own sound-effects!

LEFT HAND HERE

The Mecha-Mosquito Attacked.

RIGHT
THUMB
HERE

The Mecha-Mosquito
Attacked.

FLIP-O-RAMA 2

(pages 201 and 203)

Remember, flip *only* page 201.
While you are flipping, be sure
you can see the picture on page 201
and the one on page 203.
If you flip quickly, the two
pictures will start to look like
<u>one</u> *animated* picture.

Don't forget to add
your own sound-effects!

LEFT HAND HERE

Ricky's Robot
Fought Back.

RIGHT
THUMB
HERE

Ricky's Robot
Fought Back.

FLIP-O-RAMA 3

(pages 205 and 207)

Remember, flip *only* page 205.
While you are flipping, be sure
you can see the picture on page 205
and the one on page 207.
If you flip quickly, the two
pictures will start to look like
<u>one</u> *animated* picture.

Don't forget to add
your own sound-effects!

LEFT HAND HERE

The Mecha-Mosquito Battled Hard.

RIGHT
THUMB
HERE

RIGHT
INDEX
FINGER
HERE

The Mecha-Mosquito
Battled Hard.

FLIP-O-RAMA 4

(pages 209 and 211)

Remember, flip *only* page 209.
While you are flipping, be sure
you can see the picture on page 209
and the one on page 211.
If you flip quickly, the two
pictures will start to look like
<u>one</u> *animated* picture.

Don't forget to add
your own sound-effects!

LEFT HAND HERE

Ricky's Robot
Battled Harder.

RIGHT
THUMB
HERE

Ricky's Robot
Battled Harder.

FLIP-O-RAMA 5

(pages 213 and 215)

Remember, flip *only* page 213.
While you are flipping, be sure
you can see the picture on page 213
and the one on page 215.
If you flip quickly, the two
pictures will start to look like
<u>one</u> *animated* picture.

Don't forget to add
your own sound-effects!

LEFT HAND HERE

Ricky's Robot Saved the Day!

RIGHT
THUMB
HERE

Ricky's Robot
Saved the Day!

CHAPTER 11

Justice Prevails

The Mecha-Mosquito
had been destroyed, and
Ricky Ricotta's Mighty
Robot was victorious.

Mr. Mosquito crawled out
of his damaged ship and began
to cry. "What a bad day I am
having," cried Mr. Mosquito.
"It's about to get worse,"
said Ricky.

Ricky's Mighty Robot picked up Mr. Mosquito and dropped him into the Squeakyville jail.

Then Ricky and his Mighty
Robot flew home for chocolate
milk and grilled cheese
sandwiches.

"You boys have saved the world again," said Ricky's mother.

"Yes," said Ricky's father.
"Thank you for sticking together
and fighting for what was right!"
"No problem," said Ricky . . .

. . . "that's what friends are for."

HOW TO DRAW RICKY

1.

2.

3.

4.

5.

6.

7.

8.

9.

10.

11.

12.

HOW TO DRAW RICKY'S ROBOT

1.

2.

3.

4.

5.

6.

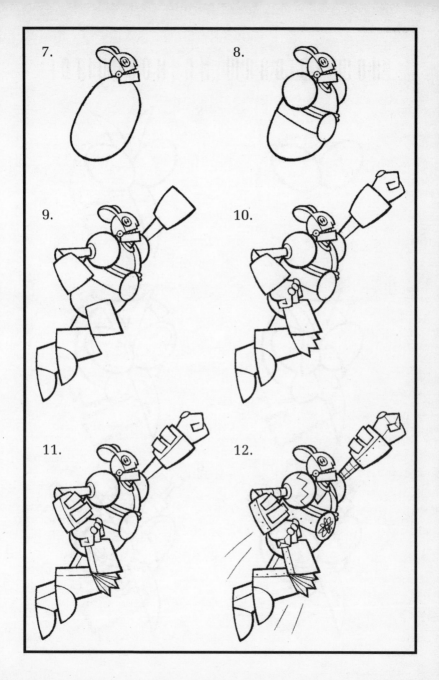

HOW TO DRAW MR. MOSQUITO

1.

2.

3.

4.

5.

6.

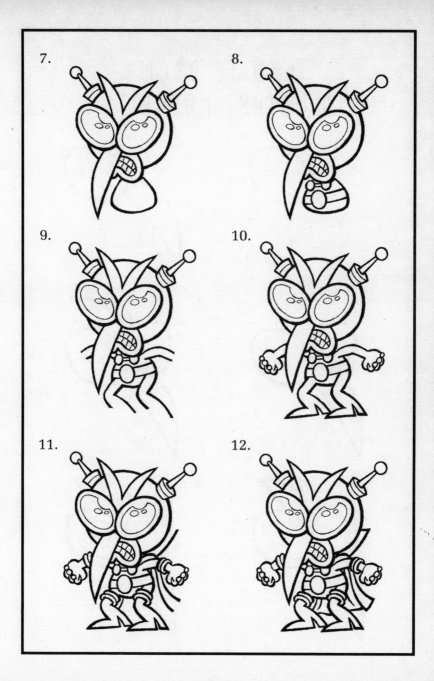

HOW TO DRAW
A MUTANT MOSQUITO

1.

2.

3.

4.

5.

6.

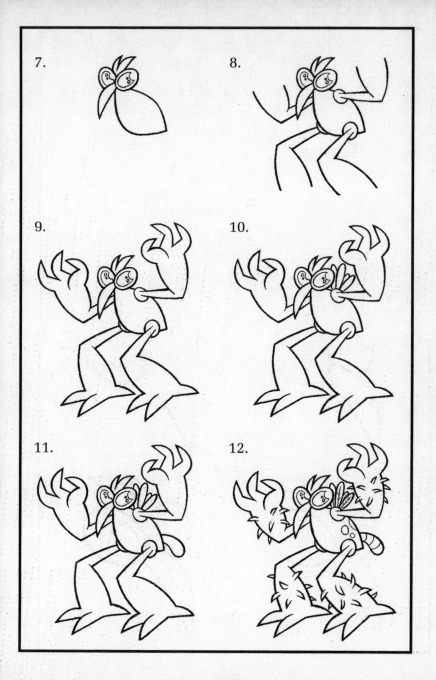

Ricky Ricotta's Mighty Robot vs. the Voodoo Vultures from Venus

Originally published as RICKY RICOTTA'S GIANT ROBOT VS. THE VOODOO VULTURES FROM VENUS

For Justin Libertowski—D. P.

To Bwana, Chloe, Trixy, and Guy—AND
especially Micki and our little expected young'un—
we can't wait to meet you!—M. O.

Chapters

CHAPTER 1

Late for Supper

It was supper time at the Ricotta home. Ricky's father was sitting at the table. Ricky's mother was sitting at the table. But Ricky was not sitting at the table.

And neither was his Mighty Robot.

"It is six o'clock," said Ricky's father. "Ricky and his Mighty Robot are late for supper again."

Just then, Ricky and his Mighty Robot flew in.

238

"Sorry we are late," said Ricky.
"We were in Hawaii collecting
seashells."

"You have been late for supper three times this week," said Ricky's mother. "No more TV until you boys learn some responsibility."

"No TV?" cried Ricky. "But *Rocket Rodent* is on tonight. Everybody on Earth will be watching it!"

"Everybody but you two,"
said Ricky's father.

CHAPTER 2

Responsibility

That night, Ricky and his Mighty Robot went to bed early. They camped in the backyard under the stars.

"I sure wish we could watch TV tonight," said Ricky.

Ricky's Robot unscrewed his hand, and out popped a big-screen television.

"No, Mighty Robot," said Ricky. "We're not allowed. We've got to learn some responsibility first."

Ricky's Mighty Robot did not know what "responsibility" was.

"Responsibility," said Ricky, "is doing the right thing at the right time."

Ricky and his Mighty Robot
were pretty good at doing
the right thing . . .

. . . but they had trouble
with the *right time* part.

CHAPTER 3

Victor Von Vulture

At that very moment, almost twenty-five million miles away, there lived an evil vulture on the planet Venus.

Temperature: 864 degrees. . . Only 2,915 hours till sunset. . . Today's forecast: mostly gassy (with a chance of sulfuric acid)

His name was Victor Von Vulture, and he hated living on Venus.

It was so hot on Venus
that everyone's food was
always ruined. Their toasted
cheese sandwiches were always
way too gooey . . .

. . . they had to drink their candy
bars with straws . . .

. . . and everybody's ice cream melted before they could even get one lick!

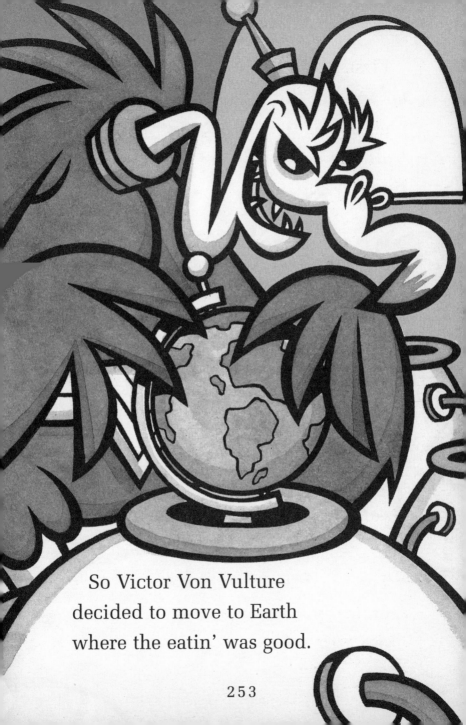

So Victor Von Vulture
decided to move to Earth
where the eatin' was good.

First, he gathered
an army of the
biggest Voodoo
Vultures he could
find.

Then he invented a voodoo
remote controller and pointed
it at Earth.

"When I press this button," said Victor, "an evil voodoo beam will shoot through space. And when it reaches Earth, the planet will be OURS!"

"Hooray for the bad guys!" cried
the Voodoo Vultures from Venus.

CHAPTER 4

Voodoo Rays from Outer Space

Ricky and his Mighty Robot fell asleep under the stars, while everyone else in town was watching television.

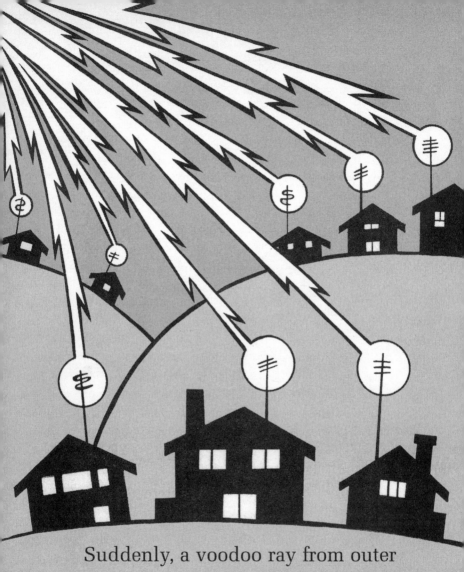

Suddenly, a voodoo ray from outer space beamed down through the night sky. The strange signal was picked up by all the TVs in town.

The screens began to glow eerily as a strange voice came from the wicked signal.

"Obey the Voodoo Vultures!" said the voice. "Obey the Voodoo Vultures!"

Soon, every mouse in the city was hypnotized.

CHAPTER 5

Breakfast with the Robot

The next morning, Ricky woke up and went inside to fix breakfast. But all the food in the house was gone.

"Hey!" said Ricky. "Where's all the food? I can't go to school without breakfast!"

Ricky's Robot knew just what
to do. He flew straight to Florida.
A few seconds later, he returned
with an orange tree.

"Thanks, Mighty Robot," said
Ricky. "I love fresh-squeezed orange
juice! Now may I have a doughnut?"

Ricky's Mighty Robot flew off
again. Soon he returned with
some fresh doughnuts.

"Hey!" Ricky laughed. "I said
a doughnut . . . not a doughnut
store! Please put that back, and
bring me some milk!"

Ricky's Robot flew away again.
This time he returned with the
freshest milk he could find.

"Ummm . . ." said Ricky. "I
think I'll skip the milk today!"

CHAPTER 6

Obey the Voodoo Vultures

After breakfast, the Mighty Robot flew Ricky straight to school. But something was not right!

All the mice in school had
strange looks on their faces.
They were all carrying food
out the cafeteria door, straight
to the center of town.

Ricky found his reading teacher,
Miss Swiss.

"What's going on here?"
asked Ricky.

"Obey the Voodoo Vultures,"
said Miss Swiss.

Then Ricky saw his math teacher,
Mr. Mozzarella.

"Aren't we supposed to have a test
today?" asked Ricky.

"Obey the Voodoo Vultures," said
Mr. Mozzarella.

Finally, Ricky found Principal Provolone.

"Where is everybody going with all this food?" asked Ricky.

"Obey the Voodoo Vultures," said Principal Provolone.

Ricky was not getting any
answers.

"Come on, Robot," said Ricky.
"We've got to get to the bottom
of this!"

CHAPTER 7

Those Vicious Vultures

Ricky and his Mighty Robot followed the long line of mice to the center of town. There, they saw a horrible sight!

A small army of giant vultures
had taken over the city and turned
everybody into voodoo slaves.
The hungry vultures were eating
every bite of food in town.

"We want more chocolate chip cookies!" yelled one of the vultures.

"Yesss, Masters," said the mice as they scurried off to start baking.

"And no more *rice cakes*!" yelled another vulture.

"We've got to stop those evil vultures," Ricky whispered. "But how?"

Ricky and his Mighty Robot looked around. They saw Victor and his evil invention.

"I'll bet those vultures are controlling everybody with that remote control," said Ricky. "We've got to get it away from them." But that was going to be tricky.

The remote control was right in the center of town where all the vultures could keep an eye on it.

"Hmmm," said Ricky. "What we need is a *distraction*."

CHAPTER 8

Ricky's Recipe

Ricky and his Mighty Robot hurried back to school. In the cafeteria kitchen, Ricky mixed some flour and milk in a large bowl. Then he added sugar, eggs, and chocolate chips.

"Now comes the secret ingredient," said Ricky.

The Mighty Robot flew straight
to Mexico and returned with the
hottest peppers he could find.

Ricky stirred the cookie batter while his Mighty Robot added hundreds of SUPER RED-HOT CHILI PEPPERS to the mix.

The Mighty Robot quickly baked
the cookies with his microwave
eyeballs, then cooled the pan with
his super-freezy breath.

CHAPTER 9

Dinner Is Served

Ricky and his Mighty Robot
returned to the center of town.
Ricky pretended he was hypnotized
as he bravely carried his cookies
toward the Voodoo Vultures.

"It's about time!" said one of the
vultures.

"Gimme those cookies!" said
another.

The greedy vultures were fighting
over Ricky's cookies. They stuffed
them into their mouths as
fast as they could.

Suddenly, the vultures' eyes got
very big. Their faces turned bright
red, and steam came out of their ears.

"OUCHIE! OUCHIE! *OUCHIE!*"
screamed the vultures as they danced
around in pain.

288

The vultures were distracted, so Ricky's Mighty Robot reached for the remote controller.

He grabbed the evil invention in his mighty fist and crushed it with one powerful squeeze.

Suddenly, all the mice in town returned to normal. They screamed at the sight of the Voodoo Vultures, and everybody ran straight home. Ricky's Mighty Robot had saved the city . . . but Victor Von Vulture had other plans.

CHAPTER 10

Ricky's Bright Idea

Victor Von Vulture grabbed Ricky
with his claw. "Don't come any closer,
Mighty Robot," said Victor, "or I will
destroy your little friend!"

The Voodoo Vultures were very angry. They huffed and they puffed as they surrounded Ricky's Mighty Robot.

"You're going to be sorry you tricked us!" said Victor Von Vulture as he flew higher and higher.

Just when everything seemed
hopeless, Ricky had an idea.

He reached up and grabbed a
feather from Victor Von Vulture's rear
end. Ricky yanked the feather out.
"*Ouch!*" yelled Victor.
Ricky wiggled the feather under
Victor's claw.

"H-hey! S-s-stop that! It tickles!"
laughed Victor Von Vulture.

But Ricky did not stop. He wiggled
the feather faster and faster. Victor
began laughing harder and harder.

Finally, Victor Von Vulture
let go of Ricky. The little mouse
fell through the air. . . .

CHAPTER 11

Robo-Rescue

Ricky was in big trouble. He was falling through the sky, faster and faster.

"Help me, Mighty Robot!" Ricky cried.

With lightning speed, the
Mighty Robot's arm shot up into
the air. The Mighty Robot caught
Ricky by the back of his shirt . . .

. . . and set him down safely in a tree. "Thanks, buddy," said Ricky. "Now go get 'em!"

CHAPTER 12

The Battle Begins

The Mighty Robot flew up and grabbed Victor in his mighty fist.

"Help, Voodoo Vultures, HELP!!!" yelled Victor.

Suddenly, the evil Voodoo
Vultures got ready to attack. The
Mighty Robot was outnumbered.

"This is going to be fun,"
Victor snarled.

The Voodoo Vultures began
to attack.

The Mighty Robot defended
himself.

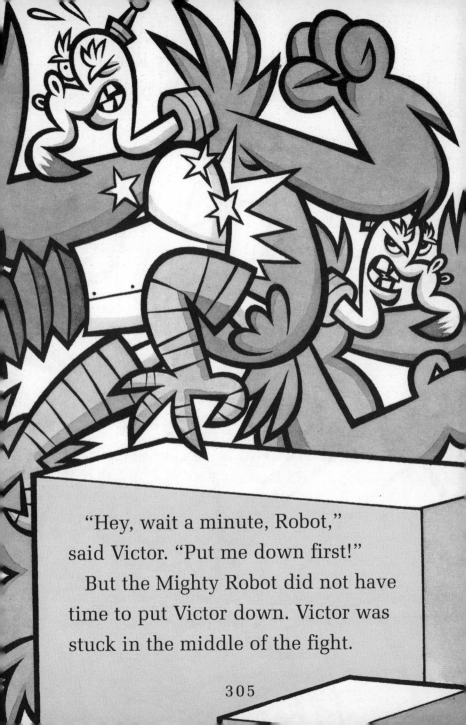

"Hey, wait a minute, Robot," said Victor. "Put me down first!"

But the Mighty Robot did not have time to put Victor down. Victor was stuck in the middle of the fight.

Every time the Mighty Robot
punched, Victor felt the blow!

Every time the Mighty Robot
clobbered, Victor got clobbered,
too!

Every time the Mighty Robot clunked heads, Victor got the worst of it!

"Ouchie, ouchie, *ouchie!*" cried Victor Von Vulture. "This is not as much fun as I thought it would be!"

CHAPTER 13

The Big Battle

(IN FLIP-O-RAMA™)

D-RAMA

HERE'S HOW IT WORKS!

STEP 1

Place your *left* hand inside the dotted lines marked "LEFT HAND HERE." Hold the book open *flat*.

STEP 2

Grasp the *right-hand* page with your right thumb and index finger (inside the dotted lines marked "RIGHT THUMB HERE").

STEP 3

Now *quickly* flip the right-hand page back and forth until the picture appears to be *animated*.

(For extra fun, try adding your own sound-effects!)

FLIP-O-RAMA 1

(pages 317 and 319)

Remember, flip *only* page 317.
While you are flipping, be sure
you can see the picture on page 317
and the one on page 319.
If you flip quickly, the two
pictures will start to look like
<u>one</u> *animated* picture.

Don't forget to add
your own sound-effects!

LEFT HAND HERE

The Voodoo Vultures
Attacked.

RIGHT
THUMB
HERE

The Voodoo Vultures
Attacked.

FLIP-O-RAMA 2

(pages 321 and 323)

Remember, flip *only* page 321.
While you are flipping, be sure
you can see the picture on page 321
and the one on page 323.
If you flip quickly, the two
pictures will start to look like
<u>one</u> *animated* picture.

Don't forget to add
your own sound-effects!

LEFT HAND HERE

Ricky's Robot
Fought Back.

RIGHT
THUMB
HERE

RIGHT
INDEX
FINGER
HERE

Ricky's Robot
Fought Back.

FLIP-O-RAMA 3

(pages 325 and 327)

Remember, flip *only* page 325.
While you are flipping, be sure
you can see the picture on page 325
and the one on page 327.
If you flip quickly, the two
pictures will start to look like
<u>one</u> *animated* picture.

Don't forget to add
your own sound-effects!

LEFT HAND HERE

The Voodoo Vultures
Battled Hard.

RIGHT
THUMB
HERE

RIGHT
INDEX
FINGER
HERE

The Voodoo Vultures
Battled Hard.

FLIP-O-RAMA 4

(pages 329 and 331)

Remember, flip *only* page 329.
While you are flipping, be sure
you can see the picture on page 329
and the one on page 331.
If you flip quickly, the two
pictures will start to look like
<u>one</u> *animated* picture.

Don't forget to add
your own sound-effects!

LEFT HAND HERE

Ricky's Robot Battled Harder.

RIGHT
THUMB
HERE

Ricky's Robot Battled Harder.

FLIP-O-RAMA 5

(pages 333 and 335)

Remember, flip *only* page 333.
While you are flipping, be sure
you can see the picture on page 333
and the one on page 335.
If you flip quickly, the two
pictures will start to look like
<u>one</u> *animated* picture.

Don't forget to add
your own sound-effects!

LEFT HAND HERE

Ricky's Robot
Saved the Day!

Ricky's Robot
Saved the Day!

CHAPTER 14

Justice Prevails

The evil Voodoo Vultures were no match for Ricky Ricotta's Mighty Robot. "Let's get out of here!" moaned the vultures.

"Hey, wait for *ME*!" cried Victor
Von Vulture. But it was too late.
The Voodoo Vultures flew back
to Venus and were never heard
from again.

The Mighty Robot picked up Ricky, and together they took Victor Von Vulture to the Squeakyville Jail.

"Boo-hoo-hoo!" cried Victor.

"Maybe now you will learn some responsibility!" said Ricky.

Then Ricky Ricotta and his Mighty
Robot flew straight home . . .

. . . just in time for supper.

CHAPTER 15

Supper Time

Ricky's mother and father had cooked a wonderful feast for Ricky and his Mighty Robot.

"Oh boy!" said Ricky. "TV dinners! My favorite!"

"We're both very proud of you boys," said Ricky's mother.

"Thank you for doing the right thing at the right time," said Ricky's father.

"No problem," said Ricky . . .

HOW TO DRAW RICKY

1.

2.

3.

4.

5.

6.

HOW TO DRAW RICKY'S ROBOT

1.

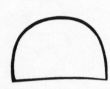

2.

3.

4.

5.

6.

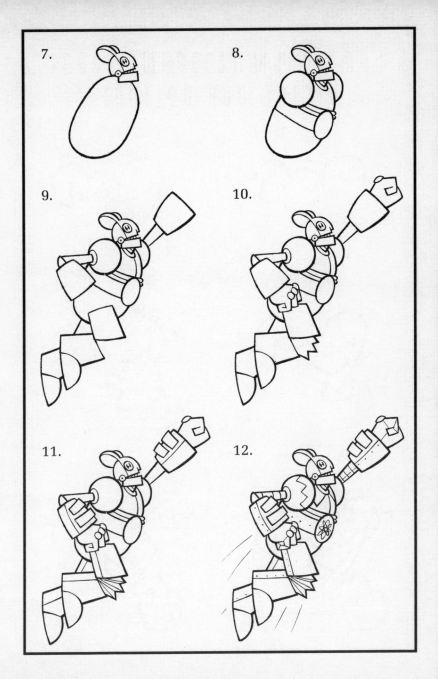

HOW TO DRAW
VICTOR VON VULTURE

1.

2.

3.

4.

5.

6.

7.

8.

9.

10.

11.

12.

HOW TO DRAW
A VOODOO VULTURE

1.

2.

3.

4.

5.

6.

7.

8.

9.

10.

11.

12.

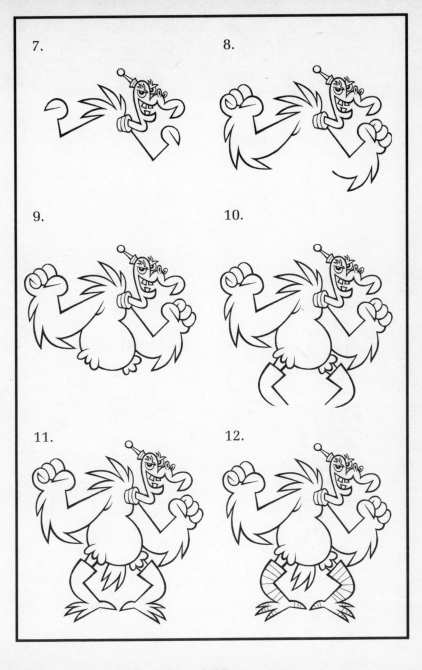

The Ladybot

The next day, Ricky ran out to the
garage where his Mighty Robot slept.

"Mighty Robot!" cried Ricky. "You
got a present! You got a present!"

Ricky's Robot threw off his pajamas
and ran to see the giant present.

"I wonder who it is from?" asked
Ricky.

Ricky's Mighty Robot opened up the present.

Inside was a giant Ladybot.

She was big and silver, and she had a giant heart on her chest.

Suddenly, the giant heart opened up and a laser beam shot out. It zapped Ricky's Robot right in his eyes.

"Hey!" shouted Ricky. "What's the big idea?"

The giant heart closed back up again, and the Ladybot returned to normal. But Ricky's Mighty Robot was not normal anymore. He had changed. He had a funny look in his eyes. He was *in LOVE*!

The Ladybot held out her hand,
and Ricky's Mighty Robot took it.
Then, together, the two Robots turned
and skipped away down the street.

BOOM! BOOM! BOOM!

"Mighty Robot!" called Ricky.
"Come back here!"

But Ricky's Mighty Robot was gone.

Will Ricky and his Mighty Robot
ever be reunited?
And can Ricky keep the solar system
safe without his big best friend?

Find out when you read
Ricky Ricotta's Mighty Robot vs.
the Uranium Unicorns from Uranus!

About the Author and Illustrator

DAV PILKEY created his first stories as comic books while he was in elementary school. In 1997, he wrote and illustrated his first adventure novel for children, *The Adventures of Captain Underpants*, which received rave reviews and was an instant bestseller—as were all the books that followed in the series. Dav is also the creator of numerous award-winning picture books, including *The Paperboy*, a Caldecott Honor Book, and the Dumb Bunnies books. He and his dog live in Eugene, Oregon.

It was a stroke of luck when Dav discovered the work of artist **MARTIN ONTIVEROS**. Dav knew that Martin was just the right illustrator for the Ricky Ricotta's Mighty Robot series. Martin has loved drawing since he was a kid. He lives in Portland, Oregon. He has a lot of toys, which he shares with his young son, Felix.

DON'T MISS RICKY'S OTHER ADVENTURES:

Ricky Ricotta's Mighty Robot vs.
the Jurassic Jackrabbits from Jupiter

Ricky Ricotta's Mighty Robot vs.
the Stupid Stinkbugs from Saturn

COMING SOON:

Ricky Ricotta's Mighty Robot

vs.

The Naughty Night Crawlers from Neptune

The Un-Pleasant Penguins from Pluto